TH

WHEN THE GAME PLAYS YOU

She Played to Win—Until the Game Played Her

Justine Robertson-Richard

Empoword Publishing Worldwide
17127 Wax Rd Ste A
Greenwell Springs, LA 70739
www.EmpowordPublishing.com
(225) 412-3130

THE COME UP by Justine Robertson-Richard
Published by Empoword Publishing Worldwide
Copyright © 2025 by Justine Robertson-Richard
The Come Up: When The Game Plays You
by Justine Robertson-Richard

Printed in the United States of America. All rights reserved solely by the author. The author guarantees all artwork and contents are original and do not infringe upon the legal rights of any other person, entity, or work. The author further guarantees that any content that is not original is rightfully and truthfully cited to the best of the author's knowledge and/or used with permission. No part of this book may be reproduced in any form without the permission of Empoword Publishing Worldwide and the author. The views expressed in this book are not necessarily those of the publisher.

This book has been edited by **Empoword Editing** located in Baton Rouge, LA (225) 412-3130.

This book is protected by the copyright laws of the United States of America. The scanning, uploading, and distribution of this book or any part thereof via the Internet or any other means without the permission of the publisher or author is illegal and punishable by law. Please purchase only authorized editions and do not participate in or encourage the electronic piracy of copyrighted materials.

The purpose of this book is to educate, motivate, and inform the reader. The author and publisher shall have neither liability or responsibility for anyone(s) with respect to any loss or damage caused, directly or indirectly, by the information contained in this book. Unless otherwise noted, all scriptures referenced in this book are in The Holy Bible New King James Version Copyright © 1982 Thomas Nelson, Inc., Publishers. The author has emphasized some words in Scripture quotations in bold, italics, or plain text.

Paperback ISBN: 979-8-317-15291-8

TABLE OF CONTENTS

Chapter 1 New Beginnings 1

Chapter 2 The Game Begins 7

Chapter 3 Settling In.. 12

Chapter 4 The Rival 18

Chapter 5 Cracks in the Façade 23

Chapter 6 Confrontation 28

Chapter 7 The Decision 34

Chapter 8 The Fall 39

Chapter 9 The Setup 44

Chapter 10 The Trap.. 49

Chapter 11 The Truth Unfolds 55

Chapter 12 Karma Comes Full Circle 61

Chapter 13 The Fall of Sandra... 66

Epilogue: The Cost of Ambition 71

Epilogue - The Road Ahead 75

CHAPTER

1

NEW BEGINNINGS

Sandra stood on the corner of Peachtree Street, her suitcase at her feet, a crumpled bus ticket clutched tightly in her hand.

The city stretched before her, alive and untamed, its skyline a jagged silhouette against the bruised hues of twilight. Glass and steel gleamed under the setting sun, and the air pulsed with energy—fast-moving traffic, hurried conversations, distant music spilling from open doors. Atlanta wasn't just a place; it was a force, humming with opportunity and danger in equal measure.

She inhaled deeply, tasting the city's essence—the rich aroma of fresh bread from a nearby bakery, the sharp tang of exhaust, the lingering scent of hot pavement cooling under the night air. A breeze lifted strands of her dark hair, sticking to the sweat at her temples. The heat clung to her, but it was nothing compared to the oppressive weight of New Orleans, where the air had felt heavy with failure.

Her heart pounded in her chest, an erratic rhythm echoing her anticipation. The moment stretched, thick with unspoken promises. *This is it.*

"New city, new hustle," she whispered, the words tasting of steel and resolve.

She rolled her shoulders back, shaking off the last ghostly tendrils of doubt. There was no room for hesitation. She had spent too many nights trapped in a cycle of what-ifs—second-guessing, trying, failing. But now, she wasn't just running from something—she was running toward something.

Power. Stability. Control.

Her fingers clenched tighter around the bus ticket, her mind flashing back to the cramped shotgun house she'd left behind—the peeling paint, the ceiling fan that rattled but barely cooled the room, the eviction notices piled on the counter like a silent accusation. The quiet hunger of a life lived in survival mode.

She was done surviving. She was ready to win.

A cab approached, its tires skidding slightly as it pulled up to the curb. The driver, a middle-aged man with tired eyes and a five o'clock shadow, barely looked at her as she slid into the backseat.

"Where to?" His voice was low, rough with exhaustion.

Sandra's fingers traced the edge of her purse as she stared out the window. She could feel the city's pulse beneath her skin—fast, electric, promising. The skyline loomed in the distance, but she wasn't headed there. Not yet.

"The Silver Star Casino," she said evenly.

The driver gave a slight nod, as if he had heard it a hundred times before. Without another word, he merged into the flow of traffic, leaving behind the quiet promise of fresh starts and plunging her headfirst into the city's undercurrent.

The Silver Star stood like a beacon on the outskirts of town, its neon lights flickering in garish shades of red, gold, and blue. The building wasn't particularly grand—nothing like the polished casinos in Vegas—but it carried the same energy. A place where fortunes were won and lost in moments. Where desperation and recklessness intertwined.

Sandra stepped out of the cab, the air thick with cigarette smoke and anticipation. The sound of slot machines jingling, the low murmur of conversation, the occasional burst of laughter or curses—it was a symphony of vices.

As she strode inside, the scent of money and desperation hit her like a wave. The air was laced with expensive cologne, stale beer, and the artificial coolness of an overworked air conditioner. The dim lighting was designed to keep people lost in time, seduced by the endless potential of the next bet.

She moved through the crowd like a lioness surveying the herd. She wasn't here to gamble—not in the way these people were. She was here to play a different game. One where the stakes were real.

And then, she saw him.

Seated at the bar, nursing a glass of bourbon, was a man who exuded the kind of wealth she was looking for. He wasn't young, nor was he particularly handsome—balding, stocky, with a thick gold watch peeking from beneath his tailored cuff. But it wasn't about looks. It was about presence.

He carried himself with the confidence of a man who was used to getting his way.

Perfect.

Sandra took her time, ordering a drink and pretending to scan the crowd. She knew exactly what she was doing—every movement, every glance, calculated.

She let her eyes find him again, just long enough to make him notice before looking away, feigning disinterest. The hook was set.

Sure enough, minutes later, he made his move.

"Hi," he said, his voice smooth, confident. "I'm Lee. Mind if I join you?"

Sandra turned slightly, allowing a slow smile to spread across her lips. She let a beat of silence linger before responding—just enough to make him want the answer.

"Sure," she said, tilting her glass toward him. "I'm Sandra. But you can call me San."

Lee signaled the bartender, ordering another bourbon before turning his full attention to her.

"San," he repeated, as if testing how it felt on his tongue. "Nice to meet you. You new in town?"

Sandra swirled the liquid in her glass, pretending to hesitate, letting the air between them thicken.

"Something like that."

He chuckled, taking a sip of his drink. "Something like that, huh? That's a vague answer."

She shrugged, giving him a coy look. "Maybe I like to keep a little mystery."

Lee smirked, intrigued. "I can respect that." He glanced her over, his eyes lingering just long enough. "So, what brings you to a place like this?"

Sandra leaned in slightly, resting her elbow on the bar. "I like to be where things happen."

"That so?" He studied her now, his interest deepening. "And what kind of 'things' are you looking for?"

She tilted her head, allowing just the faintest hint of amusement to touch her lips.

"The kind that don't come easy."

Lee exhaled through his nose, nodding. "I get that. Nothing worth having comes easy."

Sandra raised an eyebrow. "And what is it you have that was so hard to get?"

A flicker of pride crossed his face. "I own a few businesses."

She feigned curiosity. "What kind of businesses?"

"Real estate, mostly. Some investments here and there." He took another sip of bourbon. "I make things happen."

Sandra tapped a manicured nail against her glass. *Interesting.*

"I like that," she murmured, locking eyes with him. "A man who makes things happen."

The energy between them shifted—subtle but undeniable. She could feel it. The way his body language changed, the way he leaned in just a fraction more. He was taking the bait, drawn into the carefully spun web she was weaving.

But this was only the beginning.

Sandra wasn't here to play small.

She was here to win.

And by the time she was done, Lee wouldn't know what hit him.

CHAPTER

2

THE GAME BEGINS

Sandra leaned back in her chair, the soft fabric of her black dress smoothing against her skin as she took a slow sip of her drink. The dim lighting of the bar cast a warm, golden hue over the space, the air thick with the scent of whiskey, cigars, and the faintest trace of desperation. The hum of conversation swirled around her like an undulating wave, punctuated by occasional bursts of laughter, the sharp clinking of glasses, and the chime of a distant slot machine.

But Sandra wasn't here for the ambiance.

She was here for him.

Lee settled into the seat beside her, his movements deliberate, his presence commanding. Not because of his height or his build—he was solid but not imposing—but because of the way he carried himself, like a man who had already won. There was a stillness about him, a quiet confidence that spoke of power—the kind that didn't need to be flaunted.

Sandra had seen men like him before. Men who expected the world to bend to their will. But what set Lee apart wasn't just the money or the aura of influence that clung to him like expensive cologne. It was the way he watched her, studied her, as if he were trying to figure her out.

She let him look. Let him wonder. Let him think he had the upper hand.

Lee ordered another round of drinks, barely needing to signal the bartender, who moved swiftly to pour two fresh glasses of whiskey. The ice cubes clinked together in Sandra's glass as she swirled the liquid, watching the amber waves shift beneath her fingertips.

Lee finally spoke.

"So, tell me, San," he said, the nickname rolling off his tongue like he was testing the weight of it. "What brings you to Atlanta?"

Sandra tilted her head slightly, as if considering the question. She had her answer prepared, but she didn't want to seem rehearsed.

"I told you," she said, her voice smooth, her tone just a shade above casual. "I'm looking for a fresh start. New city, new opportunities." She let her gaze drift over the bar before meeting his eyes again. "I've had my fill of... old places. Old people."

She saw the flicker of understanding in his eyes, a hint of curiosity. He was interested, but he wasn't the type to take things at face value.

"I know the feeling," he admitted, rolling his glass between his fingers. "Atlanta's a city of possibilities—if you know how to play your cards right. I came here years ago to build something. Thought it was going to be easy. Turns out, it's not always that simple."

Sandra's lips curled slightly, her expression knowing.

"Nothing worth having ever is," she murmured, her voice light but intentional.

Lee chuckled, the sound warm but edged with something deeper. "You've got that right." He leaned back, studying her in the low light. "But you seem like someone who's used to overcoming obstacles."

Sandra took another sip of her drink, allowing the pause to stretch between them. She had heard this before—men who thought they understood her, who thought they could read her.

But Sandra wasn't an open book.

She was the author, and she decided what page anyone got to see.

She let a soft smile touch her lips. "I've had to be." Her voice dipped slightly, carrying just the right amount of weight. "Life doesn't always hand you the best cards. But you play the hand you're given, don't you?"

Lee's gaze sharpened. "You know, I've always believed that people like you—smart, capable, and beautiful—don't end up in situations where they have to struggle. You're not the type who gets left behind."

Sandra blinked, feigning surprise, but inside, she was smiling. She knew this game. Flattery disguised as insight. A subtle push to see how much of herself she'd reveal.

"Is that so?" she asked, her voice light, teasing.

Lee's lips twitched. "You'd be surprised. But I can tell—you don't just get by. You thrive."

Sandra let the compliment settle over her like silk. She wasn't foolish enough to let it sway her, but she understood its purpose. He wanted to see if she'd lean into it, if she'd let herself be drawn in.

She allowed herself a small, knowing smile. "I've had my share of struggles," she admitted, tilting her glass slightly. "But I always find a way to make it work. I've got my sights set on what's next."

Lee's expression shifted, something flickering behind his eyes. Interest. Respect. Curiosity.

"I think I might be able to help you with that," he said, his voice softer now, more deliberate.

Sandra's pulse remained steady, but she knew—this was the moment she had been waiting for. The opening. The first real step toward something bigger.

She tilted her head slightly. "Help me?" she asked, feigning curiosity. "How do you mean?"

Lee leaned in just enough to make the conversation feel intimate, his voice dipping lower. "I have connections, San. I know people who can open doors." He let the words hang between them, their weight unmistakable. "But you've got to be willing to take the opportunity when it comes."

Sandra's fingers traced the rim of her glass.

A test.

That's what this was. A way for him to see if she was bold enough, smart enough, hungry enough.

She met his gaze without hesitation. "I'm not the type to settle for less," she said, her voice steady.

Lee's eyes darkened slightly, his expression unreadable. But Sandra could feel it—the shift.

The moment he saw her not just as a woman at a bar, but as someone valuable. Someone worth investing in.

"I can see that," he murmured. "And I think you're exactly what I need, San."

Sandra felt the power of those words settle between them. It wasn't just an offer.

It was an invitation.

The night stretched on, their conversation slipping between business and personal, but Sandra never lost focus. Every word, every glance, every calculated pause was another step forward—another brick in the foundation she was laying.

By the time the drinks were finished and the bar had begun to thin out, Sandra knew one thing for certain—

She had Lee exactly where she wanted him.

CHAPTER

3

SETTLING IN

Sandra stood in the doorway of her new apartment, the key Lee had given her still clutched tightly in her hand. The space was small but spotless, with polished hardwood floors, modern fixtures, and a balcony that offered a partial view of the Atlanta skyline. She stepped inside, inhaling the fresh scent of new paint mixed with faint traces of the cleaning solution used before her arrival.

For the first time in what felt like forever, Sandra let herself breathe. *Really* breathe. No more cramped shotgun house in New Orleans. No more overdue rent notices piling up. No more neighbors arguing through paper-thin walls at all hours of the night. This wasn't just an apartment—it was a promise. A foothold into the life she had always wanted, and more importantly, the life she deserved.

Lee had been clear when he handed her the keys.

"I've paid the rent for the next six months. Just focus on getting yourself settled," he had said, brushing aside her protests with a wave of his hand. *"Consider it a gift."*

Sandra knew better than to believe in simple generosity. Nothing in this world came for free. But she had smiled at him, nodded at the gesture, and now—here she was.

She dropped her suitcase near the door and walked through the living room, her heels clicking against the hardwood as she took it all in. The apartment wasn't huge, but it was elegant in its simplicity—sleek countertops, stainless steel appliances, a small but stylish bedroom with plush carpeting beneath her feet. She ran her fingers along the cool granite of the kitchen island, letting the sensation sink in.

She had played the game right. And for once, she was winning.

Sandra settled onto the couch, stretching out as she let her head rest against the cushion. Outside, the hum of Atlanta's nightlife pulsed through the streets below. She could hear the distant roar of an engine, the chatter of people on the sidewalk, the faint bass from some club down the block. The city had its own rhythm, a constant movement that she was finally a part of.

Her phone buzzed. A message from Renee.

Renee: *You really left just like that?*

Sandra smirked, tapping her fingers against the screen before replying.

Sandra: *Girl, I hit the jackpot. Got me a place in ATL, and this man I met is paying for everything.*

The dots appeared instantly—Renee typing.

Renee: *Don't play with folks like that, San. It always comes back around.*

Sandra exhaled, rolling her eyes.

Sandra: *Don't hate. I've been through enough. It's my time to win.*

Renee didn't respond right away, and Sandra didn't feel like waiting for her judgment. She tossed her phone onto the couch and leaned back, staring up at the ceiling.

She had done what she had to do. And if Lee wanted to spoil her, who was she to stop him?

That night, Lee stopped by with dinner—steak and lobster from a high-end downtown restaurant. The aroma filled the apartment as Sandra met him at the door, her face lighting up with a warm smile.

"You didn't have to do all this," she said, accepting the bag of food and placing it on the kitchen counter.

"Nonsense." Lee leaned against the counter, watching her unpack the containers. *"I told you, I want you to feel taken care of. You deserve it."*

Sandra glanced at him, feigning hesitation before offering a soft smile. *"You're too good to me."*

Lee chuckled, shaking his head. *"It's not about being good to you, San. It's about seeing you happy. That's all I want."*

Sandra bit her lip, lowering her gaze as if the words meant something deeper to her. She knew exactly what he was doing—playing the role of the generous benefactor, the savior. It was almost too easy to let him believe he was rescuing her.

She turned her attention to the food, opening the containers and setting out their meal. *"You've already done so much for me,"* she said, her voice laced with gratitude. *"I don't know how I'll ever repay you."*

Lee reached out, his hand brushing against hers briefly. *"You don't have to repay me. Sometimes, you meet someone and just... know they're worth it."*

Sandra forced herself to blush, letting her lips curl into a shy smile. *"Thank you, Lee. I mean it."*

He smiled back, his gaze lingering on her before stepping away. *"Alright,"* he said, his tone light again. *"Let's eat."*

They sat together on the couch, eating from the expensive containers, sipping red wine that he had brought along. Lee talked about his business—real estate investments, side ventures, the network of people he moved with in Atlanta. Sandra listened carefully, nodding and laughing at all the right moments.

Inside, though, her mind was working furiously.

He's comfortable. He likes the idea of being needed.

She could see it in the way he looked at her, in the way he leaned in slightly when she spoke. He wanted to be the provider. The man who swooped in and changed her life. And Sandra? She would let him believe that.

Lee studied her for a moment, swirling his wine glass between his fingers. *"So, tell me something,"* he said. *"What's the endgame for you?"*

Sandra tilted her head. *"What do you mean?"*

"I mean... this. Atlanta. The fresh start. What do you really want out of all this?"

It was a test. She could feel it. A chance for him to gauge where she stood.

She let the silence stretch for just a second too long before answering. *"I just want stability,"* she said finally. *"I want to be in a place where I don't have to constantly fight to keep my head above water."* She took another sip of wine, letting her shoulders relax. *"I don't need to be rich, I just want to be in control of my own life."*

Lee watched her carefully. *"Control is a powerful thing."*

Sandra met his gaze. *"It is."*

A slow smile crept onto his lips. *"I like that about you."*

The words hung between them, charged with unspoken meaning. Sandra knew she had passed whatever test he had just given her.

The night continued with more conversation, more drinks, but Sandra never lost sight of the bigger picture. Lee was giving her everything she needed—a place to live, financial security, and the illusion of safety.

But she knew better than to get comfortable.

Because nothing in this world came without a price.

And when the time came to pay it, Sandra would make sure the cost wasn't hers to bear.

CHAPTER 4

THE RIVAL

Lee had invited Sandra to another networking event, this time with an added sense of urgency. "It's important," he had said, his voice low but carrying a weight Sandra recognized. There was something deeper at play. "You need to meet the right people, make the right connections. This could be your chance to move up in this city. We both could."

Sandra hadn't hesitated. Opportunities like these didn't come often, and she was nothing if not strategic. For weeks, she had played the part of the devoted girlfriend, but tonight, the real game was about to begin.

The event was at a high-end art gallery in Buckhead, one of Atlanta's most prestigious neighborhoods. As they entered,

Sandra took a slow breath, absorbing the luxurious atmosphere. The gallery buzzed with well-dressed investors, entrepreneurs, and high-powered executives, all mingling over champagne and delicate appetizers. Abstract art adorned the walls, seamlessly blending with the city's wealth and excess. This was where connections were forged, deals struck, and fates altered over whispered conversations and clinking glasses.

Sandra knew she belonged here. She had navigated the high society of New Orleans, but this—this was another level. A world she was stepping into with calculated precision, each move a stepping stone to the power she intended to claim.

Lee's presence was immediately noticed. His confident stride, the subtle sheen of his tailored suit, the commanding way he held himself—he was a magnet for attention. Sandra, ever the professional, stayed a step behind, allowing him to lead, letting him bask in the role of the powerful, well-connected man he was. For now, she played the silent partner.

But as they mingled, Sandra's gaze kept drifting toward a woman at the bar. Tall, striking, with raven-black hair cascading in waves down her back. Her red dress shimmered under the soft lighting, drawing the eye effortlessly. It wasn't just her beauty that stood out—it was her presence, her quiet command of the room.

Tasha.

Sandra's pulse quickened. She had seen her before, at a gala weeks ago. And while Tasha was stunning, there was something else about her—a coldness, a sharpness in her eyes that sent a jolt of unease through Sandra.

Lee noticed Sandra's lingering gaze and smirked. "That's Tasha," he said, leaning in close. "We go way back. You'll like her."

Sandra nodded, but a knot formed in her stomach. She wasn't used to feeling threatened by other women, yet Tasha exuded a quiet authority that unsettled her. She wasn't just another guest at this event—Sandra could tell. She was someone who wouldn't take kindly to Sandra's presence in Lee's life.

As if sensing the scrutiny, Tasha turned, her gaze locking onto Sandra's. Sandra straightened, instinctively composing herself. Her smile was polite but didn't reach her eyes. She refused to show weakness. Not now. Not in front of Lee.

Tasha approached, her movements smooth, calculated. Lee grinned, extending a hand. "Tasha, it's been too long."

Her eyes flicked from Lee to Sandra, assessing. Her smile was warm, but the calculation behind it was unmistakable. "Lee," she purred. Then, turning to Sandra, she offered a brief, almost dismissive nod. "And you must be Sandra."

It wasn't a greeting. It was a claim. Sandra felt the weight of it settle on her chest.

"Nice to meet you," Sandra replied, her voice steady despite the sharp, tingling awareness in the air.

Tasha studied her a moment too long. "Nice to meet you too," she said, but the unspoken challenge was clear.

Sensing the tension, Lee laughed, clapping his hands together. "Well, now that introductions are out of the way, how about a drink?"

The evening unfolded like a chess match. Tasha lingered close to Lee, engaging him in conversation, laughing too loudly at his jokes, her hand brushing his arm in a way Sandra couldn't ignore. Every time Sandra tried to get a moment alone with Lee, Tasha slipped in smoothly, like a shadow, making her feel like a spectator in her own game.

After an hour of polite competition, Sandra excused herself, stepping onto the balcony for air. The city sprawled before her, lights twinkling like stars. But her mind raced, tangled with frustration and resentment.

What is she really after?

Footsteps approached. Sandra turned to see Tasha, a glass of champagne in hand, her expression calm, almost amused.

"You know," Tasha said, her voice cool, laced with condescension, "I've been watching you all night. You don't belong here, Sandra."

Sandra's breath caught, but she kept her face neutral. The words weren't an accusation. They were a statement of fact, as if Tasha could see right through her, peeling back layers Sandra had worked so hard to construct.

"I'm not sure what you mean," Sandra said, her voice smooth but firm, betraying none of the storm beneath.

Tasha took a slow step forward, the sharp click of her heels echoing in the night air. "You see, Lee and I have history. We've known each other a long time. I just want to make sure you understand that I don't take kindly to people who think they can come in and take what's mine."

Sandra's pulse quickened, but she held her ground. She had learned long ago that standing tall, even when every part of her wanted to shrink, was the key to survival.

"I don't want anything from Lee that he's not willing to give," she said evenly. "But you might want to reconsider what you think you know. Because I'm not the one you need to worry about."

Tasha's lips curled into a thin smile. "We'll see about that."

She turned and walked away, her departure as deliberate as her arrival.

Sandra remained, her heart pounding, her mind racing. Tasha was trying to intimidate her, push her out of the way. But Sandra wasn't backing down. She had worked too hard to get this far.

As the night wore on, the unease in Sandra's chest lingered. She had expected competition. But she hadn't expected someone like Tasha—confident, calculating, dangerous.

Lee had been easy to read. Tasha was something else entirely.

When Sandra finally left the event, Lee's arm draped around her waist, she couldn't shake the feeling that she had just stepped into something far more complicated than she had anticipated.

But one thing was certain.

She wasn't going to let Tasha win. Not this time.

CHAPTER

5

CRACKS IN THE FAÇADE

The days following the networking event felt like a blur to Sandra. Tasha's words replayed in her mind, the challenge hanging over her like a dark cloud. The way Tasha had looked at her—sharp, assessing, confident—unnerved her. It wasn't just the woman's beauty; it was the certainty with which she moved through the world. And that was something Sandra understood all too well.

If Tasha thinks she can intimidate me, she's got another thing coming, Sandra thought, tightening her grip on her phone as she scrolled through her contacts. I'm not backing down.

The tension between them had been palpable, but Sandra had no intention of losing this game. She had worked too hard to get to this point, and she wasn't about to let a well-heeled woman with a history with Lee derail her plans. His world was within her reach—it had just become a little more complicated.

She kept busy in the days that followed, making calls, chasing leads, and expanding her network. But something had shifted. She could feel it in the way Lee was pulling back—distracted, distant, his usual charm dimmed by an unspoken weight. The cracks in his carefully crafted facade were becoming impossible to ignore.

Sandra had learned to read him well, and she knew when he was hiding something. A sense of unease settled deep within her, an instinct whispering that the truth was about to unravel.

Then, one evening, her phone buzzed.

It was Lee.

"I need to talk to you," he said, his voice tight, stripped of its usual confidence. Sandra's heart skipped a beat, her fingers clenching around her wine glass. "Can you come to my building? We need to discuss something."

She didn't hesitate. The urgency in his voice told her this wasn't just another dinner or business update. Something was wrong.

When she arrived, the lobby was eerily quiet. The front door was unlocked, and Lee's assistant was nowhere in sight. The absence of the usual hum of activity sent a chill through her. As she climbed the steps to his office, the sterile modern decor only sharpened the tension in the air.

She knocked softly before pushing the door open. The sight before her made her stomach churn.

Lee sat behind his desk, his head in his hands, looking smaller than she had ever seen him. His shoulders slumped, his expression hollow. The man who once seemed untouchable now looked like someone standing on the edge of a steep fall.

"Lee?" Sandra's voice was steady, but her pulse pounded.

He looked up, his eyes red-rimmed, exhaustion etched into every line of his face. "San," he whispered. "I don't know how to say this, but… things have gone too far."

Her heart thudded painfully. This wasn't the Lee who had promised her the world. This wasn't the confident businessman she had been maneuvering with. This was a man unraveling. And for the first time, Sandra didn't feel pity—she felt a flicker of opportunity.

"I've tried to manage everything, but…" He swallowed hard. "I owe too much. I'm drowning. And now, it's going to pull everyone down with me."

Sandra moved closer, perching on the edge of his desk. She forced her voice to remain calm. "What do you mean? Lee, you've always had things under control."

He gave a bitter chuckle, shaking his head. "Not anymore. I've been hiding it, but the truth is—the money's gone. I've been borrowing to stay afloat, taking out more loans, covering up debts. But I can't fix this anymore."

Sandra's mind raced. This was it. The moment she had unknowingly been preparing for—the moment when Lee's empire began to crumble. Her expression remained neutral, but inside, she was already calculating her next move.

"I can help you, Lee," she said, her voice measured. "But you have to tell me everything."

Lee exhaled shakily, dragging a hand over his face. "I'm in debt to dangerous people, San. People who don't care about business deals or negotiations. They gave me deadlines. Ultimatums. I tried to pay them off, but the interest kept piling up. Now, I'm being blackmailed. There's no way out."

Sandra's pulse quickened. She thought back to the men she had overheard in Lee's building—the ones demanding money. This wasn't a coincidence. They were part of the world he had been hiding from her.

"Who are they?" she asked, her voice barely above a whisper.

Lee hesitated, eyes darting away. "I can't say. It's too dangerous."

Sandra swallowed hard. She had played a calculated game until now, but she was standing on the edge of something much darker than she had anticipated. Helping Lee would come at a cost. The question was—was it one she was willing to pay?

Suddenly, Lee's phone buzzed. He glanced at the screen and froze.

"What is it?" Sandra asked, tension coiling in her stomach.

Lee's face drained of color. "They want their money. By the end of the week." He lifted his gaze to hers, panic raw in his eyes. "This isn't just about me anymore, San. They've threatened you, too."

Sandra felt the blood rush from her face. "What do you mean?"

"They know about us," Lee said, voice shaking. "They're using you as leverage."

Her stomach dropped. Reality hit her like a punch to the gut. Lee had never been as invincible as he had led her to believe. He had been running from his problems, and now, they were coming for her too.

The days that followed were a whirlwind. Sandra kept her distance from Lee, giving him space to sort out his mess. But every time she thought she had a grasp on the situation, another piece of the puzzle fell into place. She had been right—Lee's empire wasn't built on solid ground. It was a house of cards, and the slightest gust was enough to bring it crashing down.

But Sandra wasn't going to let it drag her down with it.

She had worked too hard to get here, too hard to make her way into this world, and she wasn't about to let Lee's downfall become her own. If she played this right, she wouldn't just survive—she would come out on top.

Time was running out. Lee was growing more desperate by the hour. Whatever move she made next had to be strategic, precise. If she could outmaneuver him now, she could emerge untouchable.

And in her gut, she knew exactly what she had to do.

It was time to play the game her way—no more mistakes.

CHAPTER

6

CONFRONTATION

The days following Lee's confession were filled with tension and uncertainty. Sandra had always been able to read people, to understand their fears and motivations, but Lee was different. His vulnerability—his fear—was something she hadn't prepared for. She had always seen him as a means to an end, a tool to secure the life she wanted. But now, as the weight of his debts and the people threatening him closed in, she found herself at a crossroads.

Late that night, she paced her apartment, the cool glow of city lights casting long shadows across the floor. The pressure of the situation pressed on her chest, making it hard to breathe. She had always known that the deeper she got into this world, the more dangerous it would become. But she hadn't expected it to happen so soon. Lee had always seemed untouchable—he had given her everything she needed, and she had played the part of the grateful girlfriend. But now, it was clear he wasn't in control. And if she wasn't careful, she would be dragged down with him.

Her phone sat on the kitchen counter, its screen dim but still glowing with unread messages. She had avoided Lee's calls all day, needing space to think, to figure out how to handle the chaos he had brought into her life. But now, as she stood in the quiet of her apartment, the decision loomed over her like a storm cloud. She could leave—cut ties and walk away with whatever money she had siphoned off. Or she could stay and take control.

Take control.

She had been doing it her whole life, and she wasn't about to stop now.

A knock at the door shattered the silence. Her pulse quickened. She had known it was only a matter of time before Lee showed up again. She was ready to face him, but part of her wasn't sure if she was ready for what this encounter might mean.

When she opened the door, Lee stood there, his shoulders hunched, his usual confidence stripped away, replaced by something darker—desperation.

"San," he said, his voice strained. "We need to talk."

Sandra crossed her arms, keeping her gaze steady. "I know. But I'm not sure where we go from here, Lee."

He ran a hand through his hair, eyes filled with guilt and something else she couldn't quite place. "I don't know what to do anymore," he admitted, voice barely above a whisper. "These people... they're coming for me. If I don't pay them, I'll lose everything."

Sandra stayed silent, the weight of his words settling between them. She had thought Lee was the one holding the power, but now, it was clear he was the one who needed her. She could use this—use him—but she had to be careful.

"How much do you owe, Lee?" Her voice was calm, almost casual.

His face faltered, and he shifted uncomfortably. "Too much," he muttered. "More than I can pay back. And these people—they won't stop until I do."

Sandra's mind was already working. This was it—the leverage she had been waiting for. The control she had been silently building could now be hers. But she needed to be sure. She needed to know exactly what she was dealing with.

She stepped closer, her voice smooth but firm. "I can help you, Lee. But you have to trust me. You have to tell me everything."

Lee hesitated, then let out a defeated sigh. "It's bad, San. I borrowed from the wrong people. They know everything—about my business, my assets. They're watching me. Watching us."

Sandra's stomach churned, but she kept her expression neutral. She had suspected it, but hearing him confirm it made the reality sink in deeper. The game had changed. And she had to adapt quickly.

"Who are these people?" she asked, her voice calm but insistent.

Lee hesitated, then finally spoke. "It's not just business, San. These people... they have connections. Dangerous ones. They don't care about me. They care about power. They want everything I have—and they won't stop until they get it."

Sandra could see the cracks forming in Lee's once-confident facade. He was unraveling, and for the first time, she realized just how deep the trouble went. But she didn't flinch. She couldn't afford to.

"I can help you," she said again, more firmly this time. "But you have to stop hiding things from me. You need to tell me everything, or this won't work."

Lee ran his hands over his face, exhausted. "I didn't want you to know. I thought I could fix it. But now... I don't know if I can."

Sandra's heart softened, but only for a moment. She had never been one to pity people—not when it came to survival. She had learned early that in this world, you took what you needed, or someone else would take it from you. And now, the balance of power was shifting.

"You can fix this," Sandra said, voice low and confident. "But you have to let me in, Lee. Let me help you."

Lee met her gaze, hesitation flickering in his eyes, but there was something else too—a glimmer of hope. Or maybe just desperation. Either way, Sandra knew she had him. She could see it in the way his posture shifted, just enough to tell her he was ready to let her lead.

She reached out, placing a hand on his arm—reassuring, but firm. Calculated. "Trust me," she whispered. "We'll figure this out together. But you have to trust me."

For a long moment, Lee said nothing. Then, finally, he nodded.

"I'll do whatever it takes," he murmured. "I can't lose everything."

Sandra's lips curved into a small, knowing smile. "Then we're going to make sure you don't."

—

The next few days were a whirlwind of planning. Sandra threw herself into Lee's world, studying his finances, his business, and the people hunting him. She charmed his associates, gathered intel, pulled strings where she could.

She knew she had to keep up the act—the supportive girlfriend who wanted to save her man. But beneath that, she was calculating every move. She wasn't just helping him out of loyalty. She was doing it to secure her place at the top.

The deeper she dug, the more cracks she found. The accounts. The businesses propped up by false promises. The people he had bled dry. The leverage was hers. All of it.

A week later, she sat in Lee's office, staring at the stack of documents in front of her. The plan was in motion. She had everything she needed. The money, the leverage, the control.

Lee walked in, his face weary but resigned. "San," he said quietly. "I did what you asked. The money's being transferred. Everything's set."

Sandra didn't look up. She could feel his eyes on her, the weight of his presence, but she kept her focus sharp.

"Good," she said, her voice calm. "You've done well."

He hesitated. "And you? Are you really going to help me?"

Finally, she turned to face him, a slow smile curling on her lips.

"I'm helping you, Lee," she said. "But remember—this is my way now."

She saw the flicker of understanding in his eyes. He wasn't in control anymore.

She was.

And now, Sandra was ready to take what was hers.

CHAPTER

7

THE DECISION

The weeks following Sandra's confrontation with Lee were a whirlwind of calculation, tension, and carefully executed moves. She could feel her grip on the situation tightening, but with every step she took to solidify her position, Lee seemed to unravel further. His once-confident demeanor—the image of a man in control—had been replaced by quiet desperation. The power he once wielded, almost tangible, was slipping away. And Sandra knew he was beginning to realize just how far he had fallen.

He was no longer the man she had first met—the one who had drawn her into his world of high-stakes games and grand promises. Now, his frantic messages, laced with desperation and guilt, served as a constant reminder: Lee was no longer an asset but a liability. And Sandra hated liabilities.

One afternoon, she paced her apartment, mind spinning with possibilities, calculating her next move. The silence in the room mirrored the storm of thoughts inside her head. She had ignored Lee's texts for days, needing space to think, to strategize. But the constant buzz of her phone kept dragging her thoughts back to him.

Her phone vibrated again. With a sigh, she grabbed it without glancing at the screen. Another message from Lee. She didn't need to read it to know what it said—she had memorized the tone, the words he always used when he was on the edge.

San, we need to talk. I can't do this anymore.

The words pressed down on her chest, but Sandra didn't let it show. She stared at the screen, fingers hovering over the keyboard, considering her response. She could tell him to stop being weak, remind him that she had kept him from sinking lower than he already was. But she didn't.

Instead, she typed a quick, cold response: **Meet me at the café downtown. I'll help you figure this out.**

It was calculated. She wasn't offering comfort—she was offering control.

That evening, Sandra arrived at the café early. The familiar hum of the place felt soothing; the dim lights and soft conversations provided a momentary calm before the inevitable storm. She picked a small table near the back, facing the entrance, ensuring she had a full view—of Lee, his expression, his body language. Everything she needed to know.

When Lee arrived, he looked worse than ever. His suit was wrinkled, his tie slightly undone, dark circles shadowing his eyes. The sight gave Sandra a fleeting sense of satisfaction—this was a man losing his grip on the power he once held so effortlessly.

She greeted him with a soft smile, the kind reserved for business meetings or moments requiring manufactured sympathy. It was a well-practiced mask. "You look terrible," she said lightly, with just a touch of concern.

Lee let out a heavy sigh as he sank into the chair across from her. "I haven't been sleeping," he admitted, his voice strained. "I can't stop thinking about everything—how much I've lost, and how much worse it's going to get."

Sandra folded her hands on the table, gaze steady. She needed him to keep talking, to keep exposing the cracks. "It's not over, Lee. We can still fix this. You just have to trust me." The words felt rehearsed, but she knew they were effective.

Lee shook his head, exhaustion evident. "I don't know if I can, San. I've already made so many mistakes, and now… now it feels like I'm drowning."

She leaned forward, voice calm but firm, infused with quiet authority. "You're not drowning. You're overwhelmed. And I'm here to help. But you need to let me in, Lee. Tell me everything."

He hesitated, eyes darting toward the window as if searching for an escape. But the weight of it all was too much. Finally, he spoke in a low, almost broken voice. "I've been trying to protect you," he murmured. "I didn't want you to see how bad it's gotten. But I can't do this alone anymore."

Sandra reached across the table, placing her hand gently over his—a deliberate, calculated move. "You don't have to do it alone. That's why I'm here. But I can't help if you keep shutting me out."

Lee's shoulders slumped, his secrets pressing him down. "It's bad, San. Worse than I've let on. The debts, the deals… I've been lying to everyone, buying time. But it's catching up to me. They've started making threats. And not just to me."

Sandra's pulse quickened, though her expression remained composed. The pieces were falling into place. "What kind of threats?" she asked, voice low but insistent. She needed the full truth.

Lee's eyes held a mixture of guilt and fear. "They know about you. They've been watching us. If I don't pay up soon, they're coming after you too."

Sandra felt a cold fury rise in her chest, but she didn't let it show. Fear wouldn't dictate her next move. The game had shifted, and she needed to play it right.

"Then we don't have a choice," she said firmly. "We take control before they do."

Lee frowned, uncertainty flickering across his face. "What do you mean?"

"I mean," Sandra replied, voice steady, "we stop playing by their rules. We make our own."

Lee stared at her, doubt clouding his features. "You make it sound so simple."

"It's not simple," she admitted. "But it's the only way. If you let them dictate the terms, you'll never escape. You'll lose everything. We both will."

Lee ran a hand through his hair, the weight of it all settling in. "I don't know if I have the strength for this."

Sandra leaned in, her gaze unwavering. "Then let me be strong for you. Trust me, Lee. I've got a plan. We'll get through this together."

For a moment, Lee was silent, his trust fragile, teetering on the edge. Finally, he nodded, though uncertainty lingered in his eyes.

"Alright," he whispered. "I'll do whatever it takes."

Sandra smiled, but it didn't quite reach her eyes. This wasn't over—it was only beginning. The cracks in Lee's empire were widening, and the weight of their choices loomed. Sandra had chosen her path: careful manipulation, calculated risks.

She would be the one left standing. No matter the cost.

CHAPTER

8

THE FALL

That evening, Sandra arrived at the wine bar early, her mind buzzing with the possibilities of how the meeting with Mark might unfold. She slid into a booth in a dimly lit corner, a vantage point that allowed her to observe the room while maintaining a sense of control. After ordering a glass of red wine, she sat back and waited, her fingers lightly tapping the table. The air carried the faint aroma of aged wood and expensive liquor—a fitting backdrop for the conversation she knew was coming.

She couldn't help but feel a small sense of satisfaction as she looked around. This was one of her favorite places—quiet, elegant, with just enough noise to obscure a private conversation. It had been a while since she'd felt this sure of herself. The game was shifting in her favor, and she was ready to capitalize on it.

Mark entered a few minutes later, his stride purposeful but not as confident as usual. His sharp suit was perfectly tailored, but his expression gave him away—he was tense, perhaps even unsettled. The careful facade that once shielded his discomfort was crumbling. Sandra noted the way his eyes darted around the room, betraying a hint of unease. It was subtle, but she caught it.

He spotted Sandra and made his way to the booth, sliding in across from her without a word. The silence between them was thick, but Sandra didn't mind. She took a slow sip of her wine, savoring the taste as she studied him.

"You're looking intense," she said, her tone light but edged. "What's on your mind?"

Mark leaned forward, elbows resting on the table. His voice was low, almost a whisper, as though the walls had ears. "The investors are worried. They've been hearing rumors about Lee's financial problems. Missing money. Unpaid debts. It's bad."

Sandra set her glass down, her expression unwavering. "Rumors always circulate when someone's vulnerable. It's nothing new."

"This isn't just talk," Mark snapped. "I've seen the numbers myself. Something isn't adding up. Investors are pulling back. If this keeps up, there won't be anything left to save."

Sandra let the silence hang, her eyes locking onto his with an intensity that made him squirm. She had learned early in life that letting someone stew in their frustration often revealed more than words ever could. Finally, she spoke, her tone calm— dangerously so. "Lee's been struggling for years. He's made reckless decisions, borrowed money he couldn't repay, and now it's all catching up to him. You know that as well as I do."

Mark's jaw tightened, but he didn't argue. Instead, he shook his head, as if trying to clear away the frustration. "What I don't know is how we fix this. You're close to him. You've been handling things behind the scenes. What's the plan?"

Sandra tilted her head slightly, tracing the rim of her glass with her finger. "The plan is simple: we take control. Lee can't fix this—he's in too deep. But we can. With the right moves, we stabilize the company and protect the investors. But it's going to take more than waiting for Lee to figure it out."

Mark narrowed his eyes. "Take control? Are you suggesting we go behind his back?"

Sandra leaned in, her voice dropping to a conspiratorial tone. "I'm suggesting we do what's necessary. Lee is already out of his depth. He's going to drown, and if we don't act, he'll take all of us with him."

Mark studied her, the weight of his decision hanging in the air. Sandra was confident. He had no other choice. Finally, he sighed, shoulders slumping slightly. "You think the investors will back this? That they'll trust you to take over?"

"They already do," Sandra said smoothly, her lips curving into a small, confident smile. "I've been addressing their concerns, keeping them calm. They see me as the one holding this together. If you back me, they will too."

Mark sat back, still sharp-eyed but now tinged with resignation. "You make it sound easy," he muttered.

"It's not," Sandra replied, firm. "But it's the only way. If you're willing to take a chance, we can turn this around. We can salvage what's left and ensure the investors come out ahead. But we have to move now."

Mark tapped his fingers against the table, jaw working as though chewing on her words. "And Lee?" he asked finally. "What happens to him?"

Sandra's smile faded, replaced by a cold, pragmatic expression. The choice was clear. "Lee is a sinking ship. He's beyond saving. The sooner we cut ties, the better."

Mark hesitated, then nodded slowly, his gaze distant as he considered the consequences. "Alright," he said quietly. "I'll back you. But if this blows up, I'm not taking the fall."

"You won't have to," Sandra assured him, lifting her glass in a mock toast, her eyes never leaving his. "Trust me. I've got it under control."

Mark didn't look convinced, but he returned the gesture, clinking his glass against hers. "Let's hope you're right."

The rest of the conversation was filled with logistics—next steps, key investors, and managing the fallout. Sandra spoke with calm authority, weaving her plans with precision. She could see Mark's doubt lingering, but he was already too deep into this to back out.

As Mark left the bar, Sandra sat back, finishing her wine, her thoughts turning inward. Mark was on board, and the investors would follow. But controlling Lee—that was the real challenge. His paranoia was growing, and she couldn't afford for him to start asking the wrong questions. His unraveling had to happen on her terms.

As she stepped into the cool night air, Sandra allowed herself a brief moment of satisfaction. The pieces were falling into place. But deep down, she couldn't shake the feeling that something was shifting beyond her control.

She had control—for now. But in this game, control was an illusion. The next move could unravel everything. And she wasn't sure if she was ready for the fall.

But there was no turning back now.

CHAPTER

9

THE SETUP

The following days felt like a race against time. Every move Sandra made had to be calculated, every conversation delicately maneuvered to maintain the fragile balance of control she'd fought to secure. Lee's paranoia was growing, and though she had managed to pull Mark and the other investors onto her side, the specter of Lee's unraveling loomed large in her mind.

Her apartment had become her command center. Spreadsheets, legal documents, and notebooks cluttered every surface. Late one evening, she sat at the dining table, her laptop casting a pale glow on her face as she typed furiously. The plan was in motion, but it required precision. One misstep, and everything she had built could come crashing down. The weight of responsibility pressed heavily on her shoulders, but she knew how to carry it. She had been playing this game for years—mastering the art of control, manipulating those around her without them even realizing it. But now, the stakes were higher than ever. Lee's fate, her own, and the future of the investors hung in the balance.

Her phone buzzed beside her. A message from Mark.

Mark: Everything's lined up. The investors are with us. Now it's up to you.

Sandra stared at the screen for a moment before typing back: **I've got this. Trust me.**

But trust wasn't a luxury she could afford. She had learned long ago that trust was a currency, and one she rarely spent. Mark and the others might be on board for now, but their loyalty was contingent on results. If she didn't deliver, they would turn on her in an instant.

Her phone vibrated again, breaking her train of thought. A reminder from her assistant about the upcoming meeting with Lee. Sandra exhaled slowly. The clock was ticking, and her plan felt like a race against time.

That evening, Sandra met with Lee in his office. The tension in the room was palpable as she walked in, her heels clicking softly against the marble floor. Lee sat behind his desk, his posture stiff, his expression strained. He looked older than he had just weeks ago—his features drawn, his eyes tired and dull. The weight of his failures was finally showing, and Sandra could see it was taking its toll. His once-pristine appearance was now marred by sleepless nights and mounting stress. She had expected it, but seeing it up close made her realize just how close to the edge he truly was.

"You're late," he muttered without looking up, irritation lacing his voice.

Sandra didn't miss a beat. "I've been busy cleaning up your mess," she replied coolly, letting the words hang in the air. Lee's face twitched with frustration.

He sighed, his shoulders slumping as he finally met her gaze. "I know things have been bad, but it feels like I'm losing control of everything. The investors are getting restless. I can't shake the feeling that they're planning something behind my back."

Sandra moved to the chair opposite him, crossing her legs and leaning forward slightly. She studied him carefully, weighing her next words. "The investors are worried because they don't see a clear path forward. You've been holding on by a thread, and they know it."

His eyes snapped up, anger flashing. "I don't need a lecture, San. I need solutions. What do you suggest I do?"

Sandra didn't flinch. "You need to let me handle this. I've already been talking to the investors, reassuring them, making sure they don't jump ship. But if you want this to work, you have to trust me."

Lee leaned back in his chair, fingers tapping restlessly on the desk. "You've been talking to them? Without telling me?"

"Someone had to," Sandra said bluntly. "You've been too busy scrambling to keep up. They needed to see stability, and that's what I gave them."

Lee's jaw tightened, but he didn't argue. He looked down at the scattered papers, his shoulders sagging under the weight of his own failure. The silence between them was thick, heavy with unspoken truths.

"I don't know if I can keep this going, San. Every day, I feel one step closer to losing everything," Lee confessed, his voice low. The vulnerability in his tone was a stark contrast to his once-easy arrogance.

Sandra's mind raced. She had to keep him under control, prevent him from unraveling completely. If he fell apart, everything they'd worked for would collapse.

She leaned forward, softening her voice just enough to seem sincere. "You're not losing everything, Lee. You're just in over your head. That's why I'm here—to help you. But you have to let me take the lead. Let me fix this."

For a long moment, Lee stared at her, searching for something—answers, reassurance, maybe even trust. Finally, he nodded, though the tension in his face didn't ease. "Alright," he said quietly. "Do what you have to do."

Sandra smiled faintly, her mind already racing with the next steps. "You won't regret this, Lee." But deep down, she knew he was still holding something back. She needed to keep a closer eye on him.

The next morning, Sandra met with Mark and the investors at an exclusive private club downtown. The sleek, modern meeting room overlooked the city through floor-to-ceiling windows. Sandra stood at the head of the table, exuding quiet authority. The tension was thick; the investors looked to her now—not Lee—for leadership. She had them where she wanted them.

"The situation with Lee's company is worse than we anticipated," she began, her tone calm yet firm. "But we have an opportunity here. With your support, I can take over daily operations and stabilize the business. It won't be easy, but if we act now, we can salvage this."

The investors exchanged wary glances. Mark leaned back, arms crossed. "And what about Lee? How do we handle him?"

Sandra's expression remained unreadable. "Lee stays the face of the company for now. Investors and creditors need to see continuity. But behind the scenes, I'll be making the decisions."

One investor, a gray-haired man named Bennett, frowned. "You're asking us to bet on you. How can we be sure you can deliver?"

Sandra met his gaze, unflinching. "Because I already have. The reason this company hasn't imploded yet is because of me. I've been managing the fallout and keeping the creditors at bay. If you back me, I'll finish what I started."

A tense silence followed. Then Mark spoke, decisive. "I'm in. We don't have a better option."

One by one, the others nodded.

That night, Sandra sat on her balcony, sipping wine, staring at the city lights. The plan was working. She had control.

But the game wasn't over yet. Lee was still a wild card, and creditors were circling. One wrong move, and everything could crumble.

For now, she allowed herself to savor the moment. She had come this far—and she wasn't about to stop.

CHAPTER

10

THE TRAP

Sandra had spent weeks carefully pulling strings, positioning herself as the savior of Lee's crumbling empire. The investors were under her thumb, the creditors temporarily appeased, and Lee had reluctantly ceded control. But Sandra wasn't naive—she knew this delicate web wouldn't hold forever. She had seen empires fall before, always doomed by the belief that the cracks were invisible, that the foundation would never crumble.

The cracks in Lee's facade were widening. He had grown distant, suspicious. His calls to Sandra were terse, erratic. She could feel the weight of his paranoia building, and she knew it was only a matter of time before he made an unpredictable move. She had worked too hard to let him ruin everything now.

She had to control the narrative—stay ahead, always.

Late one afternoon, her phone rang. Lee.

She hesitated, then answered. His voice was sharp, strained.

"We need to meet. Tonight. The Ritz. 8 p.m. Don't be late."

Sandra's grip tightened. "What's this about, Lee? I thought we had everything under control."

"There's something I need to show you," he said cryptically. "Just be there."

Before she could press further, he hung up. A gnawing unease settled in her stomach. Something was off. Had he figured her out? Was this a trap—or just another outburst? Either way, she had to be ready.

That evening, Sandra arrived at the Ritz, her heels clicking against the marble floor. She was dressed to command attention—her black dress tailored to perfection, her makeup understated but striking. As she entered the lounge, she scanned the room, assessing potential threats. Lee's paranoia had consumed him, and she knew how dangerous a cornered man could be.

She spotted him immediately. Seated in a shadowed corner, his posture tense, his expression hard. His gaze flicked up at her approach, his eyes narrowing. There was something raw about him now, like a wounded animal. She recognized it instantly—his anger barely contained. She had to tread carefully.

"You're here," he said flatly.

Sandra slid into the chair across from him, her movements measured. "You sounded urgent. What's going on?"

Lee reached into his bag, pulled out a folder, and slid it across the table. "Take a look."

Sandra hesitated before opening it. Her stomach clenched as she scanned the documents—bank statements, emails, transfer records. It didn't take long to understand.

"These are transfers from my accounts," Lee said, his voice low, laced with anger. "All traced back to you."

Sandra's chest tightened, but she kept her expression neutral. Slowly, she closed the folder, locking eyes with him. "I can explain."

"Explain?" Lee leaned forward, his voice rising. "You've been stealing from me, Sandra. Pretending to help, while lining your pockets."

Sandra's fingers curled into a fist on the table. She had expected this—just not so soon. His fury was real, but this was a calculated move to corner her. She wouldn't back down.

"I haven't been stealing, Lee. I've been protecting myself. Do you know how close you came to losing everything? If I hadn't taken control, your company would have collapsed months ago. Everything I've done has been to keep us afloat." Her voice was calm but firm. "I did what needed to be done to save you—to save us."

"Us?" Lee scoffed. "Don't pretend this was for anyone but yourself. You lied to me, San. You lied to everyone."

Sandra exhaled slowly, keeping her composure. "I didn't lie. I did what had to be done. You were spiraling, Lee.

Reckless. I stepped in before you destroyed everything."

Lee's hands slammed against the table, the sharp sound cutting through the room. "You think I didn't notice? The investors turning against me? The way you cut me out of decisions? I trusted you, and you used me."

Sandra's voice turned cold. "You trusted me because you knew you couldn't do this alone. And you were right. You needed me. You still do."

Lee's laugh was harsh. "I needed someone I could trust. Someone who wouldn't stab me in the back the moment things got tough."

Sandra held his gaze, unwavering. "Call it betrayal if you want. But without me, you would've drowned. You know it."

Lee sat back, fists clenched on the table. His fury burned, but beneath it, Sandra saw something else—fear. His empire, the one he had built, was slipping away. And she had been the one to take control.

"It doesn't matter what you think," he said finally. "I've already spoken to the authorities."

Sandra's heart skipped a beat. "What are you talking about?"

"I filed a report." His voice was cold, final. "Fraud. Embezzlement. Everything. They're looking into it now. It's only a matter of time before they come for you."

Sandra felt her control slipping for the first time. She had always been one step ahead, the one pulling the strings. But now, the trap she had set for Lee was closing around her instead.

"You're bluffing," she said, though the words felt hollow.

Lee leaned in, voice a quiet fury. "You underestimated me, San. You thought you could play me. But I've been watching. I know everything."

Sandra's mind raced. She had to think, had to turn this around. But Lee's expression told her she was out of time. The game was over. And she had lost.

—

The next morning, Sandra sat in her apartment, staring blankly at the pile of documents on the table. Her phone buzzed with a message, but she didn't check it. Her mind reeled from the night before—from Lee's accusations, from the realization that her empire was crumbling.

She had never imagined Lee would strike back so decisively, that he would pull her down with him. She had thought she controlled the narrative. She had thought she could write her own ending.

Slowly, she forced herself to stand. If Lee had gone to the authorities, she needed to act fast. She had to disappear before they caught up to her. She wasn't one to go down without a fight. But now, the stakes had changed. This wasn't about winning. It was about escape.

She grabbed a bag, shoving clothes inside—then froze at the knock on the door.

Her breath caught, heart pounding as the knock came again, harder this time. Slowly, she moved to the peephole. Two men in suits stood outside, their expressions grim.

"Ms. Sanders," one of them called, voice firm. "This is the police. We have a warrant for your arrest."

Sandra's pulse raced. The trap had closed.

The walls were closing in. And for the first time in years, Sandra wasn't the one in control.

CHAPTER

11

THE TRUTH UNFOLDS

Sandra sat in the small, windowless interrogation room, her hands clasped tightly on the table in front of her. The air was stale, and the fluorescent lights cast a harsh glow over the metal chair where she sat. She had been there for hours, the silence stretching endlessly as she waited for what was to come. Outside, faint voices hummed, punctuated by the occasional shuffle of footsteps. Her mind raced with possibilities, but she refused to let discomfort show. She wasn't going to break. Not now.

When the door finally opened, a man in a sharp suit entered. His expression was professional yet firm. He carried a folder under his arm, which he set down on the table before pulling out a chair and sitting across from her. His gaze was steady, assessing—like a predator sizing up its prey. Sandra met it with unwavering composure.

"Ms. Sanders," he began, his voice measured. "I'm Detective Harris, the lead investigator on this case. I'm sure you've been informed why you're here, but let me clarify. We have substantial evidence linking you to multiple unauthorized transfers from Mr. Lee Harper's accounts. We're also investigating possible embezzlement and conspiracy to commit financial crimes. Do you have anything you'd like to say before we begin?"

Sandra's heart pounded, but her face remained composed, a mask of calm. "I've already told your officers everything," she said smoothly. "There's been a misunderstanding. Those transfers were part of an agreement I had with Lee. He gave me access to those funds to help stabilize his business. I was acting in his best interest."

Harris raised an eyebrow, unimpressed. He opened the folder and slid a series of documents across the table toward her. "We've spoken to Mr. Harper, and his version of events doesn't align with yours. He claims he never authorized those transfers. In fact, he believes you've been systematically stealing from him for months."

Sandra leaned back, crossing her arms as she assessed the situation. Her pulse quickened as she glanced at the documents. The evidence was damning. The walls were closing in. But she had come too far to crumble now. Exhaling slowly, she summoned the control she had spent years cultivating.

"Lee is desperate," she said, her voice steady but sharp. "His business has been falling apart for years, and he's looking for someone to blame. I've been working tirelessly to help him clean up his mess. If you dig deeper, you'll see that every transfer I made was necessary to keep the company afloat."

Harris didn't buy it. He pushed the documents closer, his eyes never leaving her face. "These transfers have been traced to accounts in your name or ones directly associated with you. That doesn't look like someone stabilizing a company—it looks like someone siphoning off funds for personal gain."

Sandra's pulse quickened. She had been careful—meticulous, even—but seeing the evidence laid out so plainly was a stark reminder that her control was slipping. Every choice she had made, every step taken to ensure her survival, was now coming back to haunt her. But she couldn't afford to show fear or weakness.

"I was trying to protect myself," she finally said, her voice steady despite the storm inside her. "Lee's creditors were breathing down his neck. Investors were on the verge of pulling out. I needed a safety net. If the business collapsed, I would've been left with nothing. Everything I did was to ensure I could survive."

Harris leaned forward, his eyes narrowing. "So, you're admitting you moved the money for personal reasons?"

Sandra's jaw tightened, her grip on the table hardening. She realized too late that her words had been a mistake. "I'm saying I acted in good faith," she corrected quickly. "Lee trusted me to manage his finances, and I made decisions based on the situation at hand. If I overstepped, it wasn't intentional."

Harris didn't respond right away. He leaned back in his chair, studying her with an unreadable expression. "You're a smart woman, Ms. Sanders," he said after a long pause.

"You've clearly been playing this game for a while. But let me give you some advice: the more you try to manipulate this situation, the worse it's going to get for you. We already have enough evidence to proceed with charges. Your best option now is to cooperate."

Sandra's mind raced. Cooperate? With what? She had spent her entire life learning how to navigate situations like this, how to turn them to her advantage. But now, the walls felt like they were closing in, and there was no obvious way out. She had always relied on staying one step ahead, but now she was trapped—and the trap had been set by someone she thought she could control. Lee.

"I've told you everything I know," she said finally, her voice calm but firm. "If you want to charge me, then charge me. Otherwise, I'd like to speak to my lawyer."

Harris studied her for another long moment before standing. He gathered the documents, slipping them back into the folder. His eyes lingered on her. "Fair enough," he said, his tone colder than before. "But this isn't going away, Ms. Sanders. The truth always comes out, one way or another."

He left the room, the door clicking shut behind him. Sandra sat there, the silence pressing down on her. Her mind was a whirlwind, but she couldn't afford to let any of it break through the façade she had carefully constructed. Not now. Not when everything was at risk.

Hours later, Sandra was released on bail, her lawyer by her side as they walked out of the police station. The cool night air hit her face, but it did little to soothe the tension in her chest. She hadn't fully processed the past few hours—the confrontation with Lee, the interrogation, the looming threat of charges. It was all too much.

"You're in deep, Sandra," her lawyer said quietly as they approached her car. "The evidence against you is solid. If you don't come up with a defense strategy soon, you're going to prison."

Sandra didn't respond. She slid into the driver's seat, gripping the steering wheel tightly as she stared at the city lights. The familiar hum of the engine did little to ease the tight knot in her chest. She had always been able to stay ahead, to control the narrative. But now, it felt like the narrative was controlling her. The threads she had woven so carefully were unraveling, and she didn't know how to stop it.

She started the car and pulled away from the station, her mind racing. Lee had turned on her, the investors were on edge, and the authorities were closing in. The empire she had built on lies and manipulation was crumbling, and she was running out of time.

But Sandra wasn't done yet. She had lost control before and fought her way back. This time would be no different. Her entire life had been about power, control, and survival. She wasn't about to let it all slip away now. She had come too far.

Her phone buzzed in the cupholder, breaking her thoughts. She picked it up and glanced at the screen. A message from Mark.

Mark: I've heard about the charges. What's your plan?

Sandra's fingers hovered over the screen. She had no plan yet, no clear strategy. But she knew one thing for sure—she wasn't going down without a fight.

She typed quickly: **I'll figure it out. Just stay close.**

With that, she put the phone down and focused on the road ahead. Whatever came next, she was ready. She always had been.

CHAPTER

12

KARMA COMES FULL CIRCLE

The days following Sandra's release on bail were a waking nightmare. The once-imposing facade she had built—her control over Lee, the investors, and the entire situation—was crumbling before her eyes. Every time her phone buzzed or her email chimed, she braced herself for more bad news. The police investigation was relentless, and Sandra could feel the walls closing in. Her empire, carefully constructed through manipulation and cunning, was no longer solid. Each day, the cracks grew wider, and she had no way of patching them up.

She sat alone in her apartment one evening, the lights dim, her laptop open on the coffee table in front of her. The documents she had reviewed a hundred times were now meaningless. The evidence against her was damning. The transfers, the shell accounts, the emails—all painted a picture of a woman who had orchestrated a calculated financial scheme for her own gain. No matter how much she tried to spin it, there was no escaping the truth: she had crossed the line. For all the moves she had made to stay ahead, she had never counted on one thing—how easily everything could slip from her grasp.

Sandra poured herself a glass of wine, but the familiar comfort of the drink did little to quell the gnawing tension inside her. Her gaze drifted to the city lights beyond her balcony window, blinking in the distance like fleeting promises of a life she might never see again. She had always thought she could outsmart anyone, that she was untouchable. But now, for the first time, she felt something she hadn't allowed herself to feel in years: regret. It settled in her chest like a heavy weight, suffocating her. Could she have avoided this? Was there another way? The doubt threatened to choke her, but she refused to acknowledge it fully.

A week later, Sandra sat in a sterile conference room at her lawyer's office, the tension in the air so thick it was suffocating. She could almost taste the oppressive silence between them. Across the table, Lee sat with his attorney, his expression cold and distant. He hadn't so much as looked at Sandra since entering the room, and she felt the weight of his betrayal like a knife in her back. She had played this game over and over, thinking she could handle anything it threw at her. But now, here she was—on the receiving end of a game she thought she had mastered.

The mediator, an older woman with a calm but firm demeanor, broke the silence. "We're here to discuss potential resolutions to avoid further litigation. Mr. Harper, would you like to begin?"

Lee finally looked up, his eyes meeting Sandra's. There was no warmth in his gaze, only a quiet anger that sent a chill through her. "There's nothing to discuss," he said flatly. "She stole from me. She manipulated me, lied to me, and now she wants to negotiate? No. She gets what she deserves."

Sandra's lawyer leaned forward, his voice calm but firm. "Mr. Harper, my client has admitted to certain missteps, but this doesn't need to escalate further. We can resolve this without dragging it through court."

Lee scoffed, leaning back in his chair. "Missteps? That's what you're calling this? She siphoned money from my accounts, lied to the investors, and nearly destroyed everything I built. That's not a misstep. That's a betrayal."

Sandra couldn't hold back any longer. "Everything you built?" she snapped, her voice sharp. "You were destroying your own company, Lee. I stepped in because you couldn't handle it. If it weren't for me, you'd have nothing left."

Lee's eyes narrowed. "Don't you dare act like you did me a favor. You weren't saving anything—you were lining your pockets while pretending to help. And now you're trying to play the victim? Unbelievable."

The mediator raised her hands, her tone firm. "Enough. If we can't have a civil conversation, we'll end this session now."

The room fell into a tense silence, the weight of their shared animosity pressing down on everyone present. Sandra clenched her fists under the table, her mind racing. She had thought she could talk her way out of this, that she could regain some measure of control. But Lee's resolve was unshakable.

He wasn't going to give her an inch. She had miscalculated, underestimated the depth of his anger and betrayal. In that moment, Sandra realized the consequences of her actions were finally catching up with her. There was no longer a way to escape them.

That night, Sandra returned to her apartment and sat on the edge of her bed, staring blankly at the floor. The confrontation with Lee had left her shaken in a way she hadn't expected. She had always been able to manipulate situations to her advantage, to find the cracks in people's defenses and exploit them. But now, she was out of options. The lies she had spun over the years were unraveling faster than she could patch them together. She had fought tooth and nail for control, only to find herself powerless when it truly mattered.

Her phone buzzed on the nightstand, and she hesitated before picking it up. It was a message from Renee.

Renee: Saw the news. What happened to you, San? This isn't the girl I grew up with.

Sandra stared at the screen, her chest tightening. She hadn't spoken to Renee in weeks, not since she had left New Orleans and started this new chapter of her life. But now, everything she had built was falling apart, and even Renee could see it. She had wanted to keep her past, her true self, hidden from the world. But it was slipping through her fingers, piece by piece. Was there any hope of redemption left for her?

For a moment, Sandra considered typing a response, but she couldn't bring herself to do it. What could she say? That she had made a mistake? That she had let her ambition blind her to the consequences? Instead, she set the phone down and lay back on the bed, her mind spinning. She had to face the truth: she had gotten herself into this mess, and now she would have to live with it.

The trial came faster than Sandra had expected. The courtroom was cold and sterile, a reflection of the emotions running through her. She sat there, her hands trembling slightly as she tried to steady herself. The weight of the proceedings pressed down on her chest, making it hard to breathe. She could feel the eyes of the room on her, each glance a reminder of her failure. The prosecution laid out their case with brutal efficiency, detailing every transaction, every lie, every piece of evidence that painted Sandra as a calculating thief. There was no denying it now. The evidence was irrefutable.

When it was her turn to speak, Sandra stood, her hands trembling as she addressed the court. She spoke about her intentions, how she had only wanted to survive, how she had seen an opportunity to fix what Lee had broken and taken it. But as she spoke, she realized how hollow her words sounded. She had let her greed consume her. She had betrayed the very people she claimed to help, and now she was paying the price.

The judge's decision came swiftly: five years in prison, restitution to the investors, and a permanent stain on her record. As the sentence was read, Sandra felt a wave of numbness wash over her. It was over. Everything she had fought for, everything she had sacrificed, was gone. As the door closed behind her, she realized the truth had finally caught up with her—and there was no escaping it.

CHAPTER

13

THE FALL OF SANDRA

Months into her sentence, the cold reality of Sandra's situation had fully set in. The once-vivid dreams of power and control that had fueled her every move were now distant memories, dulled by the monotony of prison life. She had gone from negotiating high-stakes deals in luxury hotels to scrubbing floors in a sterile, fluorescent-lit facility. The fall had been swift, brutal, and final. The bright city lights, once her domain, now seemed like a distant, unreachable dream.

Sandra spent her days going through the motions—cleaning, attending group sessions, and keeping her head down. She avoided unnecessary interactions, knowing the delicate balance of life behind bars. The prison hierarchy was just as treacherous as the corporate world she had left behind, though here, the stakes were survival, not wealth. The women around her, hardened by their own stories, had little patience for weakness. To endure, she had to stay unnoticed. Every glance, every word, every move had the potential to tip the scales of her fragile existence.

At night, in the dim glow of the overhead light, Sandra lay on the thin mattress of her bunk, staring at the cracks in the ceiling. The incessant hum of the lights was a constant reminder of her confinement. Her mind drifted to Lee and the investors. Had Lee salvaged the business? Were the investors thriving under Mark's guidance? The questions gnawed at her, but she knew she would never get answers. The world had moved on without her, leaving her alone to confront her failures.

One day, during her shift in the prison library, Sandra found herself drawn to the financial section. She hadn't touched a business book in months, the thought repelling her as it reminded her of the lies and schemes that had led her here. But today, something changed. Her fingers hovered over the spine of a well-worn volume titled *The Psychology of Power*. Something about the title struck a chord. She pulled it from the shelf, flipping through the pages as she sat at a nearby table, the quiet of the library enveloping her.

The words seemed to leap off the page: *Power without principles is a fleeting illusion. It blinds its wielder to the inevitability of consequence.* Sandra closed the book and leaned back in her chair, the weight of the sentence hitting her like a physical blow. She had spent her life chasing power, believing it to be the ultimate goal, the one thing that could make her untouchable. But now, stripped of everything, she saw it for what it was—a hollow pursuit that had cost her far more than she had ever anticipated. In the silence of her cell, the truth was inescapable. Power had come at the cost of her integrity, her relationships, and her peace of mind.

Weeks turned into months, and Sandra began to adapt to the rhythm of prison life. She took on extra shifts in the library, finding solace in the routine and the quiet. The shelves of dusty books, the sound of turning pages, the faint rustle of paper became her refuge. She read voraciously—self-help books, biographies, even fiction—anything that could offer her a glimpse of redemption, a path forward.

But as time passed, Sandra realized that true redemption wouldn't come from books. It had to come from within. And that was the hardest part. Confronting the person she had been—the manipulative, calculating woman who had used everyone around her—was not easy. But as painful as it was, it was necessary. She could no longer blame others for her downfall. It was hers alone.

One afternoon, as she shelved books, a fellow inmate named Grace approached her. Grace was older, with streaks of gray in her hair and sharp eyes that suggested she'd seen more than her fair share of life's cruelty. She had a reputation in the prison—a survivor who had navigated the worst parts of life with grit and resilience. There was an air of authority about her that Sandra couldn't help but respect.

"You've been spending a lot of time in here," Grace said, her tone casual but curious, her eyes scanning Sandra as if assessing a potential ally—or a threat.

Sandra glanced at her, then returned to the stack of books in her hands. "It's quiet," she replied simply.

Grace chuckled softly, leaning against the bookshelf. "Quiet can be dangerous. Makes you think too much."

Sandra smirked faintly. "Maybe that's the point."

Grace studied her for a moment before nodding, a half-smile tugging at her lips. "I heard about you. The woman who tried to outsmart everyone and ended up here. You know, people like you don't usually make it in places like this."

Sandra's grip tightened on the book she was holding, but she kept her voice steady. "People like me learn to adapt."

Grace tilted her head, a glimmer of respect in her eyes. "Maybe. But let me give you some advice: don't let this place strip you of who you are. You made mistakes—big ones—but you've got a mind most people in here would kill for. Use it. Figure out who you want to be when you get out of here. Because if you don't, this place will chew you up and spit you out."

Sandra didn't respond, but Grace's words lingered long after she had left. It wasn't just advice; it was a challenge.

By the time Sandra reached the one-year mark of her sentence, she had begun to rebuild herself, piece by piece. She started a financial literacy program in the prison, teaching other inmates how to manage money, avoid scams, and plan for life outside. It was a small step, but it gave her a sense of purpose. She no longer woke up thinking about how to manipulate others, how to regain control. Instead, she thought about how she could help the women around her avoid the same pitfalls.

One quiet evening, a guard approached her cell. "You've got a visitor."

Sandra frowned. Visitors were rare. Setting her notebook aside, she followed the guard to the visitation room, her heart pounding.

When she stepped inside, she froze. Sitting at the table, looking both out of place and entirely at ease, was Lee.

He glanced up as she entered, his expression unreadable. For a moment, neither of them spoke. Then Sandra moved to the table and sat down across from him.

"What are you doing here?" she asked, her voice calm but guarded.

Lee folded his hands on the table, his eyes locked on hers. "I wanted to see how you were doing."

Sandra raised an eyebrow, a bitter smile tugging at her lips. "You wanted to see if I was broken yet?"

Lee shook his head. "No. I wanted to see if you've learned anything."

Sandra's smile faded. "And what do you think?"

Lee studied her before answering. "I think you're starting to understand what it means to lose everything. But I also think you're stronger than you realize."

Sandra didn't know what to make of his words. But for the first time, she wasn't paralyzed by the fear of what came next. She wasn't just the sum of her mistakes. She could change. And maybe, just maybe, she was ready to try.

EPILOGUE:
THE COST OF AMBITION

Months into her sentence, Sandra had plenty of time to reflect on the choices that had led her here. Her cell was small, its walls stark and unyielding, and the days blurred together in a monotony that drained her spirit. She had always believed ambition was her greatest strength—that it would carry her to the life she deserved: rich, untouchable, at the top. But now, sitting on the hard cot in the dim light of her prison cell, she realized that ambition without integrity was a path to ruin. She had learned this lesson in the hardest way possible, but far too late to undo the damage.

Each day felt like a slow unraveling of the person she used to be. The sharp, calculating woman who once navigated Atlanta's high-stakes world of power and wealth was now a shadow of herself. No longer in control, no longer the puppet master, Sandra had been reduced to nothing more than an inmate—a statistic in a system that cared little for her ambition, only her crime.

In the silence of her cell, she replayed the events over and over—the lies she had told, the people she had manipulated, the friends she had betrayed. She had always prided herself on being two steps ahead, anticipating every move, controlling every outcome. But now, there was nothing left to anticipate but the relentless passage of time.

She thought about Lee—the way he had looked at her during the trial. His expression had been cold, distant. And for the first time, she had truly seen him for who he was: a man broken by his own failure, a man who had trusted the wrong person, and who now sought revenge. The weight of his betrayal lingered in her bones, but even heavier was the sting of her own actions. She had played the game and lost, but the cost of that loss was far greater than she had ever imagined.

Outside, the world continued without her. Atlanta's power brokers carried on their dealings, its high-rises still cast long shadows over streets that no longer remembered her name. The investors who once hung on her every word had moved on, and the empire she had fought so hard to build had crumbled overnight. Sandra had spent years manipulating every situation to her advantage, but it had all vanished in an instant. Now, she was nothing more than a cautionary tale—her name whispered in boardrooms as a warning of what happens when ambition runs unchecked.

Some days, she wanted to scream, to rail against the injustice of it all. But the reality was undeniable. She had made choices—self-serving, ruthless choices—and they had led her here. There was no one else to blame. She had always been the one pulling the strings, but now, she was the one caught in them.

Her thoughts often drifted to Renee. She hadn't spoken to her since her fall from grace, but now, with nothing but time to reflect, she wondered where her old friend was. Had Renee moved on? Had she found peace? Or had she, too, become collateral damage in Sandra's relentless pursuit of power?

Sandra had once believed she could control everything, but the people who had truly cared for her were the ones who had suffered the most. She had pushed them all away, blind to the destruction she was leaving in her wake.

Sometimes, in the stillness of the night, Sandra would close her eyes and picture a different life—one where she had made different choices, one where she had stayed true to herself and the people who mattered. But that life was nothing more than a fantasy, a dream she would never wake up to. The past was unchangeable, and the choices she had made had brought her here.

In this place of isolation, she had learned that true power was never about manipulation or control—it was about understanding oneself. It was about knowing when to let go and trust in something greater than ambition. But for Sandra, the lesson had come too late. The years she had spent chasing wealth and influence had come at an unbearable cost—her freedom, her dignity, her relationships.

In the end, Sandra understood that the price of her ambition had been far greater than anything she had gained. It had cost her everything she once held dear. And now, with years stretching endlessly ahead of her in a place where nothing could be controlled, she had no choice but to confront the truth: ambition had been her greatest strength, but it had also been her undoing. She had spent her life trying to outrun the consequences of her actions, but no one could run forever.

As she lay on her cot, staring at the ceiling, Sandra finally understood the full weight of her choices. She had been driven by the hunger for success, for control at any cost. But in the end, she had sacrificed herself in the process. Now, all that remained was the woman she had become—broken, repentant, and forever marked by the price of her ambition.

EPILOGUE -
THE ROAD AHEAD

The years following Sandra's release from prison were a blur of transition. No longer the ruthless manipulator she once was, she reentered the world as a stranger in a life she had once dominated. The noise and chaos of her past had been replaced by the quiet rhythm of a simpler, less dangerous—but more uncertain—existence. She wasn't the same woman who had walked through those prison gates. In the solitude of her cell, she had been forced to confront the decisions that had led her there—the choices she had made in pursuit of power, leaving her isolated and broken.

For the first time, she saw how ambition had blinded her, how her need for control had eroded the very things that could have sustained her—relationships, integrity, peace of mind. The long nights behind bars, where the outside world had seemed so distant, had given her time to reflect on the consequences of her path. She wasn't just facing a future shaped by her mistakes; she was grappling with the pain of knowing that everything she had worked for had been built on fragile ground. She had lost everything she thought mattered—power, wealth, influence. All of it, mere illusions.

But Sandra was a survivor. She had learned from her mistakes, piecing together a new version of herself—one built not on manipulation but on responsibility and redemption. The road ahead was uncertain, but she now had a clearer vision, one that no longer relied on deceit or greed but on earning back trust, starting with herself. The weight of her past still pressed on her, but she was learning to carry it—one step at a time.

The road to redemption was far from easy. It would have been simpler to succumb to the anger and resentment that threatened to consume her, to blame others for her downfall. But over the years, she discovered the power of taking ownership of her choices. She no longer denied her mistakes. She accepted them, and with that acceptance, found the strength to move forward. There were moments when the old temptations whispered to her—the familiar, intoxicating pull of power—but she resisted, knowing that going down that path again would cost her more than she was willing to lose.

Finding work was a struggle. No one was eager to hire a convicted felon, especially one with her history. After months of job searches, rejections, and interviews that led nowhere, she found a nonprofit organization that believed in second chances. It wasn't glamorous work, but it was honest. She helped people who had made mistakes—just like her—navigate the complexities of finance. She taught them how to manage money, avoid the traps she had once fallen into, and rebuild with what little they had left. It was humbling, and while she had once hoped for more, the work gave her purpose. It gave her a reason to wake up every morning.

The first few months were difficult. Sandra was still learning how to relate to people without the tactics of her past. She had to listen without dominating, to build trust without manipulation. It was a slow process. Many of the people she met at the nonprofit bore deep scars—some visible, others buried within. She recognized their brokenness because she had lived it. And she knew better than most that healing wasn't about quick fixes or empty promises.

One afternoon, while leading a workshop for at-risk young adults, Sandra noticed a familiar face in the back of the room. She froze mid-sentence, her gaze locking onto the young man sitting there. Recognition hit her instantly. He had been an inmate she once mentored in prison—quiet, observant, never saying much, but always listening.

Now, he was different. He had moved on, built a life outside, just as she had dreamed of doing.

Back in prison, Sandra had pushed him to think differently, to take control of his future. At the time, she hadn't expected much in return. But now, standing in front of him, seeing the man he had become, she felt something stir inside her—a mixture of pride and awe. He had done the work. He had built something from nothing. And, like her, he had changed.

After the session, he approached her. He looked stronger, more confident, and his eyes held a sincerity Sandra hadn't expected.

"Thank you," he said quietly, his voice thick with gratitude. "For everything you taught me. I wouldn't have made it without you."

Sandra smiled, her heart swelling with quiet pride. "You did the hard part," she replied. "You changed your own life. All I did was show you the way."

He nodded, his expression softening. "Maybe. But you gave me more than just lessons. You showed me it's never too late to start over. To do better."

His words hit Sandra deeply. It was the first time she truly felt that the work she had done—the effort she had poured into teaching others—had mattered. She hadn't built an empire, but she had built something far more valuable: a future. A future where she could help others avoid the same mistakes she had made. It was a small victory, but it was hers. And it felt like the first real win she had experienced in a long time.

As she watched him walk away, Sandra thought about the life she had once dreamed of—the empire she had wanted, the power she had chased. And then, for the first time, she realized that this new life was enough.

Building a legacy wasn't about wealth or influence. It was about impact. It was about touching lives in a way that left a lasting imprint.

It wasn't easy. There were still days when she thought about the past, about the power she once wielded, about the regrets that lingered. But those thoughts grew quieter with time. She knew now that power had never been the answer. What mattered was how she used the lessons she had learned—the wisdom carved from hardship. She didn't need to be a queen in a kingdom of her own making.

She just needed to be better than she had been.

Some nights, Sandra would sit at her small desk, reviewing case files, reflecting on how far she had come. She was no longer chasing anything. No longer running from her past. No longer seeking validation. She had learned to live without it.

Healing, she realized, wasn't about fixing everything. It wasn't about perfection. It was about finding peace within the chaos, learning to accept imperfections, and embracing the slow, steady path of growth. She no longer measured her worth by success or failure. Her worth came from how she showed up every day—how she contributed, how she learned, how she moved forward.

One morning, as she sat at her desk reviewing a new case, Sandra smiled.

It wasn't the smile of someone who had won.

It was the smile of someone who had found freedom.

For the first time in a long time, Sandra was content.

Her journey wasn't over. There were still lessons to learn, more people to help, and challenges ahead. But for the first time in years, she felt a deep sense of peace—one that came not from accolades or power, but from within.

She had found something more valuable than all of it.

She had found herself.

Made in the USA
Columbia, SC
27 April 2025